HAND in HAND

By Andria Warmflash Rosenbaum

Illustrations by Maya Shleifer

APPLES & HONEY PRESS

Note to Readers

Many children were separated from their families during the Holocaust. During this terrible time, from Hitler's rise to power in Germany until the end of World War II in 1945, millions of people were persecuted, imprisoned, and killed for being different. Ruthi and Leib's story is sewn together from accounts of Jewish children who survived, despite the odds. Some of these children were eventually reunited with family members.

Was there a key ingredient that gave these children the strength to keep going? Was it the help given to them by others who had lost everything, yet refused to surrender? Was it chance and circumstance? Did hope and faith raise the odds in their favor? I'd like to believe that for children like Ruthi and Leib, it was the love their families had planted deeply within them that helped them endure, despite separation and suffering.

Encourage children to ask questions and talk about their feelings as you read *Hand in Hand* together. Ask them if they've ever had to do something that was hard, or frightening, and how they found the strength to keep going. Follow their lead to help them explore topics they are comfortable talking about.

In loving memory of the one and a half million children
lost to the Holocaust. I will never let go.

—AWR

Apples & Honey Press
An imprint of Behrman House
Millburn, NJ 07041
www.applesandhoneypress.com

Text copyright © 2019 by Andria Warmflash Rosenbaum
Illustrations copyright © 2019 by Maya Shleifer

ISBN 978-1-68115-538-8

Designed by Maya Shleifer • Edited by Amanda Cohen

Printed in the United States of America
1 3 5 7 9 8 6 4 2

Library of Congress Cataloging-in-Publication Data is available.

Mama had a smile
sweeter than strawberries
in summer. So did my
little brother, Leib.

The fall I turned seven
Leib tumbled into four.

Then soldiers stomped
brutish boots into town
and across all our days.

They
HOVERED
OVER OUR HEADS,
LIKE TiDY ROWS
of STORM CLOUDS –
THREATENING to BURST.

Mama whispered,
"Don't worry, my doves.
Sometimes, walls rise up.
Still, there is always
a way . . . forward."

But we read the fear
echoing in her eyes.

She told us to stay together.
That she had to go to find food.

"I'll be back before you
can say goodbye,"
she promised.

She hugged us too tightly.
Pressed kisses upon our heads.
Then suddenly, like the sun

she was gone.

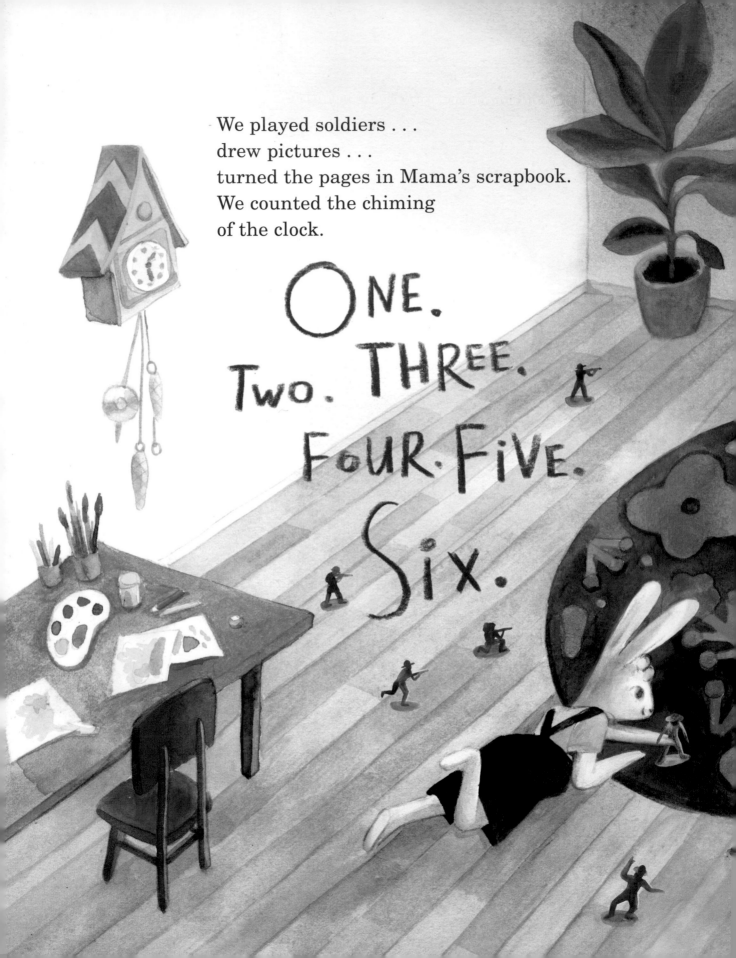

We played soldiers . . .
drew pictures . . .
turned the pages in Mama's scrapbook.
We counted the chiming
of the clock.

ONE.
TWO. THREE.
FOUR. FIVE.
SIX.

"Ruthi," cried Leib.
"I've said goodbye too many times!"

I held Leib's hand in mine.
I told him I'd never let go.

When night swallowed the light
we peeked out the window, wishing for Mama.
But she didn't return.

By morning we were hungry,
cold, and scared. I held Leib's hand
as he cried, until a neighbor came to our door.

"Please, leave a note for Mama," I begged.
But he said we had to hurry.

I grabbed some photos from Mama's scrapbook and stuffed them in my pockets. Leib and I were taken to an orphanage.

WE WERE
LEFT LIKE BOXES.

Soon Leib stopped talking.
But I never let go of his hand.

One day a couple fell in love
with Leib's blonde curls and sapphire eyes.
They wanted to take him home.

I tore a picture of us in half
and pushed the part with my face
into his palm.

I kissed both
of my brother's velvet cheeks,
but never said goodbye.

I buRied the MEMORIES
of LEiB's and MAMA's strawberry smiles
Deeply, into the center of MY HEART.

Weeks turned into months.
My world was shredded
and scattered to the wind.

I walked through Nightmares,
in a place where numbers
replaced names.

But even in that
colorless landscape
people passed me
crumbs,
pushed me . . .
forward.

A CHILD
IS HOPE,
THEY whispered.
HOPE
will LIVE,
THEY
COMMANDED.

And one spring morning
the black boots vanished.

The nightmare . . . came to a halt.

I was sent on a boat
over a wide, wild sea
to a strange, new home

Stocked with DREAMS,
Food, WATER, STRONG SUN,
And LAUGHTER.

I worked
the swampy soil,
filling, digging,
raking, clearing,
planting tomatoes,
squash, cucumbers,
and eggplant.

Slowly, surely,
I was brought
back to life.
As yellow flowers
bloomed
on each plant,
so did
I . . .

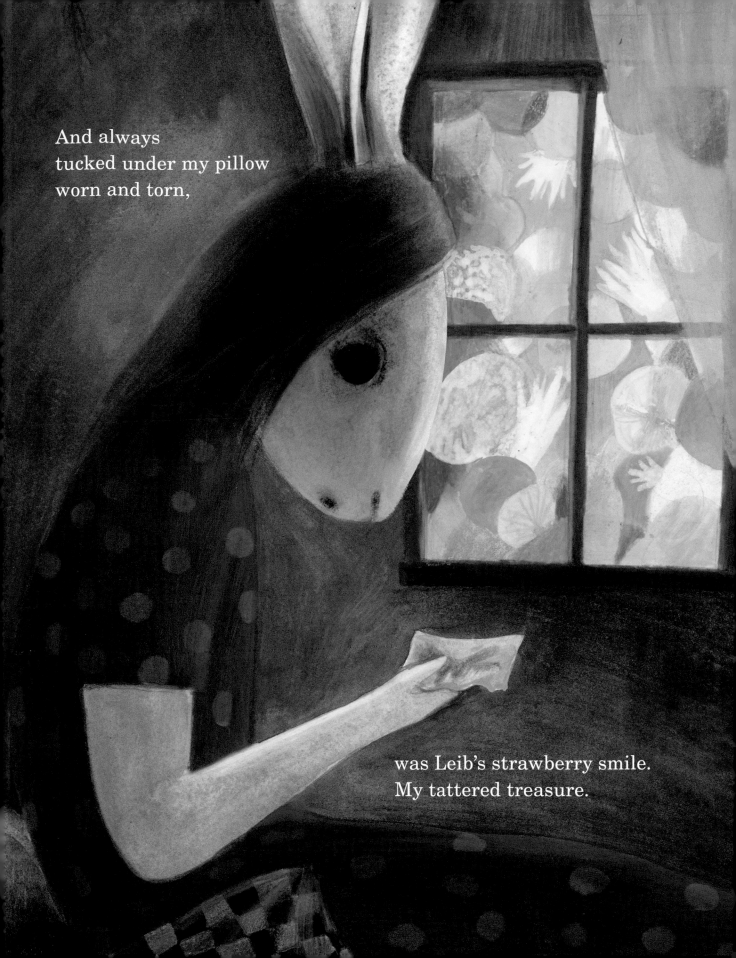

And always
tucked under my pillow
worn and torn,

was Leib's strawberry smile.
My tattered treasure.

MANY YEARS LATER,

AFTER I'd MARRIED,

MY CHILDREN

AND GRANDCHILDREN

URGED ME to add

My NAME to the Lists

of others like ME.

Children who had
their families,
their homes,
their childhoods,

TAKEN.

One of these children
found my name.
He wondered.
He called,
asking if it might
. . . be true?

COULD it be Leib? My Leib?

WHAT if it wasn't?
WOULD HE REMEMBER ME?
How Would I know if it was HiM?
RAISED IN Different COUNTRIES,
HOW WOULD WE UNDERSTAND
EACH OTHER?

On the way to meet him
I trembled.

As strangers passed
I saw an old man,
not quite as old as me.
There wasn't much left
of his thick curls,
and his chubby cheeks
were carved with age.

His blue eyes had lost
their sapphire luster,
but through my tears
my heart knew
Leib's strawberry smile.

"SHALOM,
MY BiG SiStER,
RuthI!"

Brother and sister,
heart to heart,
hand in hand,
after so many years,
after loss and pain,
finding a way forward,
keeping a promise to

NEVER LET GO.